Love and
kisses from
Great Aunt Linda
and Great Uncle Steve
2019

Counting with Barefoot Critters

by Teagan White

N
W
E
S
11
12
10
9
8

for Alex & Maribeth, and their little one

One

A quiet day reading is perfect for one.

Books take you to everywhere under the sun.

But when the story is over you might start to feel blue

And realize your day would be better with...

Two!

Pancakes are more fun to make as a pair.

They taste so much better when we can share.

Once our bellies are full, we are finally free

To go play outside in a small group of...

FLOUR

Three!

Adventures outdoors are exciting with three
We can find hidden paths or a new climbing tree.
But when we run out of new spots to explore
Maybe it's time to change it to...

Four!

Sometimes our friends have their paws full with chores

And the hard work would be much less boring with four.

If we all work together like bees in their hive

We'll be finished in no time and ready for...

APPLE

Five!

On bright sunny days we feel strong and alive

And there's no better number for racing than five.

When the winner is crowned and we've all had our kicks,

We're ready to find out what's more fun with…

Six!

The race made us hungry; it's time for a break

And there's room at the table for six to eat cake.

Laughter and food with friends is like heaven

When our plates are all clean we'll see what's up with...

7

Seven!

With seven brave pirates to sail the high seas

The dangerous quests are finished with ease.

When we've found all the treasure and rescued our mates

We can row back to shore and make our group...

Eight!

Surely we've earned a nice, peaceful rest,

Now that we've finished our daring conquest.

We nap in the garden or the shade of a pine

And later we'll wake up and gather as...

Nine!

Now that we're rested, the next thing in line
Is to visit our fort, where there's just room for nine.
We climb high in the trees to see far past our den
Then it's back down to land, and we're ready for...

10

Ten!

After skinned knees and sunburns what sounds like more fun

Than an afternoon swim to cool off from the sun?

Ten swimmers take turns in a pond fit for seven

Till our crowd moves along to make room for...

Eleven!

Eleven empty bellies after a long, busy day
Are soon filled with food round a bonfire's blaze.
The day's getting late and we've all stuffed ourselves
But we still have time left for a party of...

Twelve!

As the forest grows dark we head home for the night,

Led by our friend with good evening eyesight.

The stories are spooky and darkness is near

But with us twelve together, there's nothing to fear.

Back home and in bed you have time to reflect

On the friendships and memories your life can collect.

With other minds to inspire you and make your days fun

You'll always feel loved, even when you're just one.

Tundra Books, a division of Random House of Canada Limited,
a Penguin Random House Company

Library and Archives Canada Cataloguing in Publication

White, Teagan, author
Counting with barefoot critters / Teagan White.

Issued in print and electronic formats.
ISBN 978-1-101-91771-8 (bound).—ISBN 978-1-101-91773-2 (epub)

1. Counting—Juvenile literature.
2. Animals—Juvenile literature.
I. Title.

QA113.W458 2016 J513.2'11 C2015-903995-9
C2015-903996-7

Published simultaneously in the United States of America by Tundra Books of Northern New York, a division of Random House of Canada Limited, a Penguin Random House Company

Library of Congress Control Number: 2015947651

Edited by Samantha Swenson
Designed by Teagan White
The artwork in this book was rendered in watercolor and gouache.
The type in this book was set in Stanyan.
Printed and bound in Hong Kong

www.penguinrandomhouse.ca

1 2 3 4 5 6 21 20 19 18 17 16

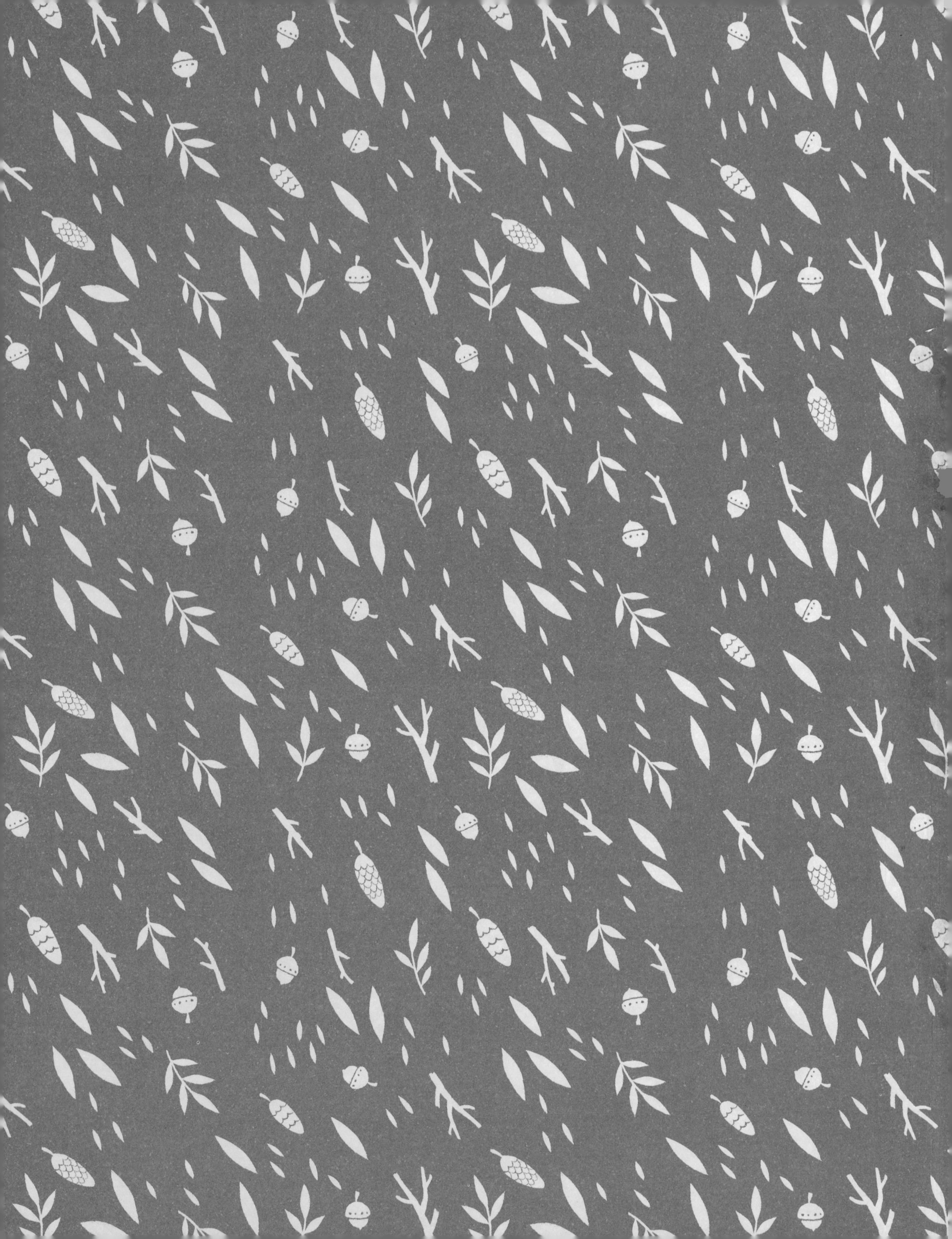